This book belongs to

_____

TO ERIEL

I AM A GREAT KID!

BY CECILIA D PORTER

I AM A GREAT KID!

I respect my parents.

I trust them and I obey them.

I AM A GREAT KID!

Above all else, I love God.

I want to love Him and He loves me.

I AM A GREAT KID!

I understand that I should give thanks to God for all things and in all things.

I AM A GREAT KID!

I understand that I should have respect
and dignity for all people.

I AM A GREAT KID!

I must show forgiveness when someone wrongs me and is against me.

I AM A GREAT KID!

I know that I will not always get my way.

That is okay. No one gets their way all of the time.

I AM A GREAT KID!

I understand that I am always growing as a Christian.

There will be good times and bad times.

I AM A GREAT KID!

I must understand the importance of prayer.

Talking to God is important.

God wants me to talk to Him.

I AM A GREAT KID!

Manners and common courtesies
are very important.

I AM A GREAT KID!

Strength is found in serving and
not in being served.

I AM A GREAT KID!

I must have compassion for the poor, homeless and needy.

I AM A GREAT KID!

Life is always a teaching moment.

It is important to be flexible and adaptable to cope with life.

I AM A GREAT KID!

I must be faithful in all things, including the little things.

I AM A GREAT KID!

My choices are mine to make.

I need to make good choices.

People will always remember the bad choices that I make.

I AM A GREAT KID!

I need to remember that life is never fair.

I will not compare my life to someone else.

I must be thankful for what God has given me.

I AM A GREAT KID!

I need to understand how to lead
and how to follow.

In order to be a good leader,

I must learn to be a good follower.

I AM A GREAT KID!

I know that LOVE conquers all.

Everybody will not be right.

Some people will be wrong and do wrong.

Regardless, I don't have to like what they do,

but I must love them regardless.

I AM A GREAT KID!

Lightning Source UK Ltd.
Milton Keynes UK
UKHW051038151220
375215UK00002B/137